THE WINTER WREN

THE WINTER WREN

BROCK COLE

A Sunburst Book · *Farrar, Straus & Giroux*

NEW YORK

For Anthea, Naomi, and Jonah

One year spring would not come.

The new wheat turned yellow and rotted in the furrows, and in the air was a taste of iron.

There was little to eat in the village, and so when Simon burned the porridge and spilled the milk, his mother was very angry.

"You daft thing!" she cried. "Can't you do anything right?"

Simon scratched his head and thought, but he couldn't be sure. "Don't be sad, Mother," he said. "You'll think of something."

His mother sighed and shook her head. "Well, why don't you climb up on the barn and watch for spring? Perhaps you can do that right." And it will keep him out of harm's way, she thought.

"But what does she look like?"

"Who?"

"Why, Spring!"

"Oh, you are a sweet befuddling fool!" And his mother laughed in spite of herself. "She must be a princess all dressed in green and gold."

But when Simon got to the top of the barn there wasn't a sign of a princess in green and gold. All that he saw were two ravens fighting over a bit of bacon rind.

"Give me a bite," begged one, "and when Spring comes, I'll find you a nice robin's egg."

"That will be never," said the other, laughing. "Spring's asleep at Winter's farm and can't wake up."

With a snip and a snap of his great black bill, he swallowed the bacon and flew away.

"So that's the way it is," said Simon, and he slid down the thatch and went to tell his mother.

"Goodbye, Mother. You'll have to manage without me for a while. There's nothing else for it."

"Where are you going?" she asked.

"Why, haven't you heard? Spring's asleep at Winter's farm and can't wake up, poor thing. I'm going to help her."

"Take me with you," said his sister Meg.

Who could say no to little Meg?

Not Simon.

Their mother didn't know what to make of such foolishness, but she gave them a small sack of meal and an apple in case they got hungry, and a kiss each for her little daughter and her great daft son.

"How will we know Spring when we find her?" asked Meg.

"She's a princess all dressed in green and gold, that's for sure," said Simon.

"Oh," said Meg, and was quiet.

With Meg on his back, Simon walked and walked, but he didn't get tired. His sister weighed hardly more than a bird.

Finally they came to a farm where nothing grew.

There was Winter, striding back and forth over his fields, sowing the earth with sleet.

"Hey, Old Winter!" called Simon. "Where is Spring? We've come to wake her up!"

But Winter would have none of that. He gave a great roar and threw a handful of ice at the two children.

Simon turned to run. Quick as he was, he was not quick enough. A hailstone hit Meg smack in the back.

There was a pop and a twitter, and Meg disappeared.

Where she had been was nothing but a tiny brown winter wren, who flew up in a tree over Simon's head.

Poor Simon sat down and began to cry.

"Don't cry, Simon," said the Winter Wren, and she flew down and sat by his shoulder. "Do as I say, and everything will come right."

Simon wiped his eyes and blew his nose. "What shall I do, Winter Wren?" he asked.

"Creep up close behind Winter, and where he sows sleet, you sow meal."

Simon did as the Winter Wren said. Wherever Winter sowed sleet, Simon spread a bit of meal from the sack that his mother had given him.

And wherever a speck of meal fell, there sprang up a fresh green stalk of wheat.

The green spikes prickled and tickled Old Winter's toes so that he danced and stamped.

"Who sows meal where I sow sleet?" he cried, twisting this way and that. But Simon kept close to Winter's back so that he couldn't be seen.

It was too much for Winter. He threw down his sack of sleet and stomped off over the fields.

"After him quickly!" cried the Winter Wren, and Simon ran as fast as he could.

Soon he saw Winter again, pruning the buds from his apple trees.

"Creep up close," whispered the Winter Wren, "and throw your apple into the orchard."

Simon did as the Winter Wren said, and where his apple touched the ground a great tree sprang up and blossomed.

When Winter touched the tree, his sickle melted, and his cold fingers burned.

"Who plants where I prune?" he cried, and turned this way and that. But Simon hid beneath the blowing blossoms, and Winter couldn't find him.

The old fellow growled and bellowed and fled into his house.

"After him quickly!" called the Winter Wren.

But the door was locked fast, and Simon could not open it.

"Blow through the keyhole," said the Winter Wren.

Simon did as he was told, and his warm breath melted the locks quite away, for Winter's locks are nothing but ice.

The door sprang open, but there was no sign of Winter. In all of his cold kitchen there was no one but a little girl spreading butter on a piece of bread.

"Hello. I've come to wake up Spring," said Simon.

"You have?" said the girl. "And will you know her when you see her?"

"Oh yes. She's a princess all dressed in green and gold."

"A princess in green and gold? That would be at the top of the stairs," said the girl, and took her breakfast into the garden.

As Simon went up the stairs he could hear the Winter Wren singing overhead, but when he reached the landing the singing stopped.

In a tiny bedroom filled with flowers was a great feather bed, and on the feather bed someone sat up and yawned.

Was it Spring?

No. It was Meg.

"Oh, Meg, there you are," said Simon, picking up his sister and giving her a hug. "But where is Spring?"

A warm wind shook the curtains and made the windows clatter, and Simon looked out.

"So that's the way it is!" he said, laughing. "Look, Meg. There she is. Wide awake now."

Down they went, out into Winter's garden, and started across the fields
for home.

Spring rolled before them like a great green wave.

When they reached their village, their mother and the other villagers were planting lettuce and potatoes.

"Spring came while you were gone, Simon," said his mother.

"I know. We woke her up at Winter's farm."

"You did, did you?" said his mother, laughing. "And was she a princess all dressed in green and gold?"

"Oh no, you were quite wrong about that," said Simon. "She was nothing but a bit of a girl, just like our Meg." And he sat his sister up on a wagon so that everyone could see just how Spring was.

The villagers all laughed, but Simon's mother gave him a hug, because she loved him even if he was a sweet befuddling fool.